Ex Líbrís

Nathan Wada

how to hide a crocodile

& OTHER REPTILES

With special thanks to
Robert C. Drewes, Ph.D.
Chairman
Department of Herpetology
California Academy of Sciences

If
you take
a careful look,
you'll see
how
creatures
in this book
are
CAMOUFLAGED
and out
of view—
although
they're
right
in
front
of
you.

RUTH HELLER'S

how to hide a crocodile

& OTHER REPTILES

Reinforced binding

Grosset & Dunlap

It's the usual style of the
NILE CROCODILE
to

bask by a river or lake for a while,

then to follow an urge to partly submerge,
so all that you see…

is
this
floating debris.

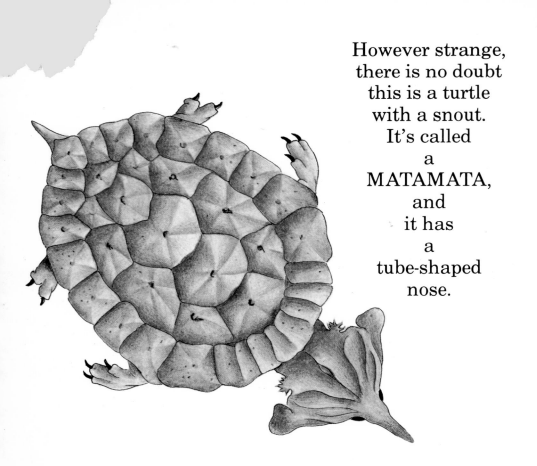

However strange,
there is no doubt
this is a turtle
with a snout.
It's called
a
MATAMATA,
and
it has
a
tube-shaped
nose.

It likes the river bottom and...

that is
where

it
goes.

So
agile
is the
GREEN TREE SNAKE
that
slender branches
do
not
break,
nor
do the bushes
quake
or
shake…

as it
weaves
among
the leaves.

This
patterned
PYTHON
predator...

lurks
on the leafy
jungle
floor.

This
IGUANA
and the
tree

bear a similarity....

If he's
hidden
will depend
on
how well their colors blend.

The
CHAMELEON's
disappearing
act
is
an
old,
established…

fact.

By
day
the
GECKO's
skin
is
light.

At
night
it
turns
quite
dark.

But either way
this lizard's skin...

looks
very
much
like
bark.